# NEST UNDER SIEGE

# NEST UNDER SIEGE

## DRAGON APPROVED™ BOOK FOUR

RAMY VANCE

MICHAEL ANDERLE

DISRUPTIVE IMAGINATION

## THE NEST UNDER SIEGE TEAM

**Thanks to the JIT Readers**

Kathleen Fettig
Misty Roa
Dorothy Lloyd
Diane L. Smith
Deb Mader
John Ashmore
Larry Omans
Angel LaVey

*If I've missed anyone, please let me know!*

**Editor**
The Skyhunter Editing Team

LMBPN Publishing
PMB 196, 2540 South Maryland Pkwy
Las Vegas, NV 89109

First US Edition, February 2020
Version 1.01, February 2020
eBook ISBN: 978-1-64202-726-6
Print ISBN: 978-1-64202-802-7

# DEDICATION

*To Hamish for helping me fail...*

*—Ramy Vance*

*To Family, Friends and*
*Those Who Love*
*to Read.*
*May We All Enjoy Grace*
*to Live the Life We Are*
*Called.*

*— Michael*

# CHAPTER ONE

Alex watched the orcs standing outside of the room through Gill's holographic display. At first, she stared at the screen through Manny's eyes, but the detail was too much. Manny saw everything. Every little hair on their chinny-chin-chin... (Seeing gave so many of the stories she knew new context.)

She switched to her own eyes, dulling the sight through her HUD.

She held her breath, trying to make as little noise as possible. It didn't matter that they were all huddled in a room. It just meant that if the orcs heard them, they were all dead.

After a few minutes, the orcs wandered away and continued on down the hall.

Alex let out a deep sigh as she leaned back against the wall and tried to catch her breath. "How many do you think there are?" she asked after she was sure she could breathe regularly.

Gill looked through his HUD, changing between different

cameras throughout the Wasp's Nest. "There could be hundreds," he murmured. "There's a lot of these guys."

Jollies fluttered around the room manically before finally going into a fit of hiccups and retiring to Alex's right shoulder. "What should we do?" Jollies asked.

Alex looked from Brath to Gill as the two young men thought the question over. Gill was the first to speak. "We should watch for a bit longer," he suggested. "It doesn't make sense to run out there until we know what's going on. I mean, if we had gone out earlier, we'd be..." He ran his finger across his neck

Alex nodded in agreement. "Yeah, you're right. If we had gone out, we'd be dead by now. There's no way we could have taken that many orcs."

"What do you mean, taken? Were you thinking about fighting them?"

Alex shook her head. She knew this wasn't VR anymore. This was real life, and real orcs were very capable of killing her.

*One-lifers. Guess we're all one of those now*, she thought with a heavy sigh.

For a moment, Alex thought back to *Middang3ard* VR. She had been a hero there, ready to step into danger at a moment's notice. People knew her throughout the game as someone who would not walk away from a fight.

Yet here she was crouched in a room with a bunch of teenage boys, shaking with fear. *How the mighty have fallen*, she thought.

Brath was pacing, his arms folded over his chest, his body language expressing how unhappy he was with the decision to stay and hide. "How long are we going to be doing this?" he asked.

Gill lowered his visor and met Brath's eyes. "It would be a mistake to go out before we have properly assessed the situation," he reminded the other rider. "Haven't you been paying attention to anything during our tactics lessons?"

Brath sat down on his bed, his arms still crossed. "Yeah, I pay attention," he muttered under his breath. "I thought the first word of that class's name was 'Battle.'"

"Yeah, it is. And the second word is 'Tactics.' Arguably, it's the more important word. Let me just see what else is going on for a while, all right? Then we'll discuss what we should do."

Alex sat back and listened to Gill. The hair on the back of her neck prickled. *Who died and made these guys the bosses?* she wondered. *They're not even asking for Jollies' or my opinion.*

Brath stood back up and continued pacing. He looked like he was going to say something else but was concentrating very hard on not speaking. His face had gone red from concentration.

Jollies, on the other hand, wasn't trying to hide how worried she was. The color of her skin kept fluctuating between deep blue and purple.

Alex tapped Jollies on the foot, hoping to distract her from her fear. Maybe distract herself as well. "Do all pixies change color like you?" Alex asked.

Jollies looked up suddenly as if she had forgotten she was resting on Alex's shoulder. "Huh? Oh, yeah. It's like an emotional thing. Kinda like how you humans have mood rings. I'm one big mood ring. It helps pixies empathize with each other. Totally inconvenient when talking to non-pixies, though. Makes lying harder. You'll never catch a pixie playing…poker? That's the human game, right?"

Alex reached over to Brath's bed, grabbed a pillow, and threw it at Gill. "Hey, do you have any cards in here?"

Gill hardly responded to being hit with a pillow. He looked away from his HUD visor for a moment before returning. "Yep," he replied. "Over there, on top of my dresser. Why?"

Alex got up and grabbed the cards. They weren't like any cards she'd ever seen in Middang3ard before. They reminded her of a description she had read of tarot cards, but other than that, they were completely confusing to her.

She took them anyway.

Brath scoffed loudly as he sat down on his bed. "Are you seriously going to play cards right now? While the Nest is going through an orc invasion?"

It took all of Alex's self-control to speak in an even tone to Brath. She was terrified, but sitting in a room thinking about how scared she was wasn't going to help anyone.

Even if Brath didn't want to admit it, Alex could tell he was afraid too. All his pacing and sitting and standing were dead giveaways. Gill was the only one in the room who didn't seem worried about the orcs.

Alex sat down across from Brath and looked at the cards. She looked at them, and even never having seen playing cards before, she knew this wasn't an Earth card deck. The images were too... She struggled for a word before settling on "fantastical."

She handed them to Brath. "Do you know what these are?"

Brath snatched the cards from Alex's hands and sighed loudly. He thumbed through the cards before handing them back to Alex. "Of course, I do," he said. "These are drow Fate cards."

"What are those?"

Brath looked taken aback by Alex's asking for more details. For a moment, he forgot about the orcish invasion and was more concerned with trying to understand why she would be interested in the cards.

Alex took the cards back from Brath as he started to

explain, "It's an elvish thing. All kinds of elves get these when they're born. Every elf gets their own specific deck—someone makes it for them or something—but they use them to tell the future. Usually their own future."

Alex nodded to show that she understood. They weren't much different from Tarot cards then. She needed to do something to wake these guys up. Jollies was in full panic mode, and Brath wasn't far behind.

Panic meant being stupid.

She shook her head. "I'm going to show you some human magic now. I'm going to read your fate."

Brath scoffed. "Humans don't have magic."

"That's not true. We humans have magic. Maybe not blow-'em-up-with-a-fireball magic, but we are powerful divinators."

Gill looked up and stared at Alex for a moment before going back to checking the camera feeds.

Brath laughed before realizing he was making noise and covering his mouth. "You didn't even know what those were a minute ago," he growled. "Why do you think you're going to suddenly know how to read my cards and my future with your human magic?"

Alex thought back to her Aunt Maisy, who used to read fortunes for fun. Maisy would read Alex's future, vividly describing the cards to her as she turned them over. When she was in *Middang3ard's* VR world, Alex had looked them up, wanting to know what Aunt Maisy had been doing. It was incredible how good Aunt Maisy's descriptions had been.

And how fun her tarot card readings had been.

Maisy had said that the most important thing with divination was confidence. You could say anything you wanted, all you had to do was sell it. Brath hadn't challenged her on the divination part, so she had a chance.

As she shuffled the cards, she did her best to channel her Aunt Maisy. She thought about how, when Maisy spoke, it sounded as if there was no doubt in her mind. "Yeah, I am going to read your fate. I used to be quite the card reader on Earth."

"How did you learn when you can't see?"

Alex looked up from the cards for a moment. She couldn't tell if Brath had said that with the intention of hurting her or if she was just sensitive due to all the prior teasing. "Special cards with ridges," Alex lied. "Just because I was blind, it didn't mean I was helpless."

"So, you read with ridges?"

"Yeah, same as with books. You get that I know how to read, right?"

Brath shrugged as he tried to look uninterested. "I hadn't thought about it," he muttered.

Alex cut the cards and then shuffled them again. "On Earth, we have a special written language called Braille. It's just for blind people. It's a series of raised dots that mean certain letters or words, and I had cards with that."

Alex watched something she had never seen before. She couldn't have put it into words even if she wanted to. Brath's face had changed slightly. It wasn't as if he had raised his eyebrows or smiled, but as she spoke, Alex saw Brath's eyes soften a little bit and his face loosen up.

Alex passed Brath the deck of cards. "All right, choose three cards," she instructed. "Any three cards you feel drawn to."

Jollies floated down and took a seat next to Alex's foot.

Brath chose three cards from the top of the deck and handed them to Alex, who took them and put them on the floor. Alex looked over her shoulder at Gill, who was watching. She winked at him before turning back to the cards.

Alex flipped the three cards and leaned over them as she clasped her hands together, her chin on her knuckles.

The first card was a raven, the second a burning building. And the third was a black circle.

Alex nodded theatrically as she picked up the first card and stared at it, pretending to draw some meaning from it. "This right here represents your past," she said mysteriously. "It looks as if your past was filled with anger. Anger about things you couldn't control."

Next, Alex picked up the card depicting the burning building. "But something changed," she went on. "There was a sudden shift, and everything fell apart. You had to start asking questions, inspecting the foundation, figuring out why things had collapsed."

Alex looked up to check if Brath was buying it.

The gnome was silent, and his brooding eyes peered out from behind his scruffy beard.

Alex took up the last card. She stared at it for some time, drawing out the anticipation. "Ah. The sacred ring is your future."

Brath leaned forward but caught himself quickly and tried to downplay his interest. "Oh yeah?" he asked.

"That means your future is…well, I guess the best way to say it is that you have infinite possibilities with where you go from here. After the past and present stuff that I said before, you get to choose what your future is after you're done asking questions."

Brath chuckled as he leaned back. "You could have said that about anything."

Alex took the three cards and put them back into the deck. "True," Alex admitted. "I could have said them to anyone. But I said them to you and only you. Right now. So, take that as you will. But I see that today will not be your last."

After shuffling again, Alex had Jollies draw cards. Hers were dove wings, dragon fire, and a skull. "Oh, that's bad," Jollies said. "The skull means I'm dead."

Alex shook her head and gave the pixie a sly smile. "No, you misunderstand. It means that you are the bringer of death." She looked at the two recruits and saw them both emboldened, their panic subsiding. Good. She had gotten through to them.

No panic meant they were thinking again, and that gave them all a chance.

Gill, the only one who had been calm the whole time, raised his finger to his lips, turned off the lights, and motioned for them all to get closer.

Gill threw up a holograph from his HUD that showed their hall. There were more orcs walking down the hall, but this time, they were kicking open every door. The orcs were only a few doors away.

Gill shifted the view to another hallway. Dead bodies covered the floor.

Alex grabbed her mouth to keep from yelping. She had never seen anything dead before. She wanted to look away more than anything else in the world.

Gill changed back to their hallway. "There's worse going on right now," he said. "Fights throughout the Nest and they're coming our way. Real soon. Any ideas?"

Brath jumped to his feet and pulled out a knife hanging from his waist. "We fight them," he whispered. "Better than sitting here and waiting for them to find us. At least we choose how we die."

Jollies was shaking her head as she tried to fight back tears. Alex could see that the pixie was terrified, and there was a part of Alex that was scared too, but she felt the same way Brath did. If there was going to be a fight, it should be on their terms.

The images of the dead cadets in the hallway flashed through Alex's mind. Her desire to fight instantly dissipated. She could be one of the corpses in the hall. Her parents would never know.

Gill stood up and turned off the holograph. He walked over to Brath and coaxed him into putting away the knife. "I know you're looking forward to using your father's blade for revenge," Gill said softly. "But there'll be a better time. We need to figure out what we're going to do to stay alive."

Alex pointed up to the unlit light bulb in the middle of the room. "Can you get into the systems and turn off the lights for the whole place?" Alex asked.

Gill looked at the lightbulb and then at the darkness of the room. "I can try."

# CHAPTER TWO

Gill attempted to hack into the entire Nest system. His brows were furrowed as he tried to figure out how to get past the firewalls. Alex wondered how such a young kid had managed to acquire that much hacking expertise.

Manny sat quietly in the corner. He hadn't spoken a word since they had been ushered out of the mess hall. Alex wondered if Manny was panic-stricken, but that seemed unlikely. It wouldn't have made sense for Myrddin to assign Manny to Alex if he spooked so easily.

The desire to walk over to the dorm room's door and peek through the peephole was overwhelming. Alex pushed it down along with her fear, which was doing its best to take over her reasoning. She kept imagining the orcs breaking into the room and tearing them all to shreds.

The lights in the hallway flickered. Alex could see light through the crack where the door didn't quite touch the floor, but they still remained on.

Outside, there was another explosion. This one was big enough to rock their room. Orcs started yelling in the hallway. Alex couldn't make out what they were saying, but she assumed that it was something violent in Orcish.

Brath sighed as he started to pace and finger the knife hanging from his waist again. Once in a while, he would stop and look at Gill, who would glance at his visor and shake his head.

Alex had never missed the HUD in *Middang3ard* so much before, not even when she was on Earth, trying to stay awake during her homeschooling lessons. The HUD she had received when she got her armor was noticeably different.

The HUDs in *Middang3ard* had an amazing feature that allowed their users to gauge what their likelihood of success or failure was going to be. All you had to do was look at a situation that you were thinking about, and the HUD gave you your success ratio.

Over the last few months in VR, Alex had become extremely dependent on that little percentage. It made all the difference in whether or not she would engage in a battle. She wished that she knew what her likelihood of survival was right now.

Gill groaned, frustration dripping from his voice when he spoke. "Damn it, there are so many back ends, I don't even know where to start. Maybe I should just try to isolate the hallways. No, that doesn't make sense..."

Alex walked over to Gill and took a seat beside him. "What if you just knocked out the whole network? Just kill the whole Nest."

Gill rubbed his cheek as he thought it over. "I guess I could do that," he admitted. "But I don't know how it's going to affect the Nest as a whole. The fact that no one has done it before makes me unsure if it's a good idea."

"No one else has done it because they don't have an ace up their sleeves like I do."

"What do you mean?"

Alex pointed to her eyes. "You kill the lights, I can lead us out of here," Alex explained. "I don't need to see anything. Old habits die hard, I guess. I've been memorizing every corridor since I've been here. I can get us around the orcs."

Brath nearly sneezed and caught himself. "Have you seen what the orcs are wearing? They have night vision for sure."

"But we have another ace up our sleeve. Manny can cast Darkness, right?"

The Beholder nodded. "I can."

"Night vision or not, they'll be blind, and unable to navigate the corridors like I can."

Brath nervously tugged on his beard. "Okay, but that only solves one problem. How are you going to get around the orcs? If we accidentally bump into one of them, we're dead."

Alex pulled out her blindfold and wrapped it around her eyes. "Trust me," she assured Brath. "I lived my entire life moving through darkness. I can do this. We get out of the room and make our way to the stables. Then we take back the Nest."

Gill and Brath exchanged glances before Brath nodded.

Taking the cue, Gill spoke up. "All right, you heard the lady. Let's do it," he said before pulling his visor back down and starting the hack.

Manny floated forward, his tentacle eyes moving about rapidly. "I'll cast Gloom. That way, it won't be total darkness. Then I'll link everyone's eyesight together so you can see through my eyes. We should be able to make each other out. That way, we can follow Alex easier, but we'll have to stick together. Real close."

Gill cleared his throat and said, "I can help too. Drows have darkvision. Mine isn't that strong since it matures with age, but I should be able to pick up on the heat signatures of the orcs if they're close by. I'll take the front with Alex. And you guys better get ready. It's going dark in three, two, one."

The lights in the hallway flickered again and then went off. There were startled sounds from the orcs outside, followed by another flurry of words that Alex couldn't make out.

Manny floated in the middle of the circle of kids. "All right," he whispered. "Jollies, Brath, you two ready?"

"Ready," they both replied.

Manny's body started to vibrate, and beams of light shot out of his eyes. The same beams shot out of Jollies' and Brath's eyes.

Brath leaned forward, his hands out in front of him, and yelped as he caught himself. He slammed his hands over his mouth and tried to keep his balance.

Gill stood up from his seat and walked over to Alex. He slid his hand around Alex's and squeezed tightly. "This way, we won't get separated," he whispered in her ear.

Alex's heart was racing. She wouldn't have thought it could have beaten any faster than when she'd first seen the orcs, but she was wrong. "Yeah, that works perfectly," she mumbled.

*Get it together, Alex,* she thought . *You can have a crush later if you survive this.*

Alex reached out as she had her entire life and inched toward the room door. She knew exactly where it was without realizing it, since her and Jollies' room was the same. *Glad to know that muscle memory didn't go to waste,* she thought as she instinctively concentrated on the door opening slowly.

The crystal door pulled apart, hardly making any noise. To the untrained ear, it was probably not even noticeable.

Alex scanned the hallway. It was a habit she'd acquired since she had been able to see, but it was pointless in this situation. She knew the orcs were close. They hadn't been too far off in the video feed.

Alex didn't need to see to know exactly where the orcs

were, though. She could smell them since they didn't smell like anything else in the Nest. A sour, acrid scent rose off of their skin, and Alex was happy she didn't have to see them up close.

It only took the slightest tug on Gill's hand to guide him. The drow stepped lightly as if the lack of light didn't bother him at all. Alex could hear Brath struggling to walk forward behind Gill.

Alex assumed that whatever Jollies and Brath was seeing, it wasn't too different than the sight Manny had first given her. It should have been more than enough to make their way through the hallway.

But Alex was saying that as someone who knew how to navigate the dark.

Brath and Jollies were probably struggling to pick up what little detail they could using Manny's vision. *You'd think for someone with so many eyes, his vision would be better, even in the dark,* Alex thought.

The smell of the orcs faded as Alex guided Gill and the rest of them down the hall. Alex had a fairly good idea of where they were. Even with how mazelike the Wasp's Nest was, she had been able to develop a sense of location and proximity by walking down the halls due to the crystal walls.

Hopefully, the confusion of the Nest would work to their advantage. Cadets had a hard enough time moving around and finding where they were trying to go. The orcs must have been having an even harder time navigating the Nest.

What were they here for, though? The only thing Alex had seen was murder. Jollies had said orcs had attacked training camps before, but was it really as simple as murdering all the new cadets? *They could be here for the dragons,* Alex thought.

But what good were dragons to the Dark One? It wasn't like any of them would have followed him, even though Alex had been told he'd had at least one dragon. Maybe he was trying to get more.

Alex squeezed Gill's hand, signaling for him to stop. They all stood very still in the darkness. She could smell orcs ahead. She knew that they were at a four-way intersection in the hallway. That made it impossible to tell which way the orcs were coming from.

Alex pulled Gill up against the wall, and Manny and the rest of them followed. They stayed there as the smell of the orcs approached.

Gill guided Alex's hand upward. He pushed down all of her fingers except for her index and pointed to the left, signaling which direction the orcs were coming from.

All five of them froze and held their breath. Alex squinted, tempted to pull off her blindfold and see if her dragon eyes granted her any abilities to see in the dark. It was too much of a risk, though. The sudden shift from being blindfolded to being able to see might be too much.

Alex didn't need to see the orcs to know they were walking past. Her nostrils filled with the smell of rancid meat and decomposing bodies. *How could any living thing smell this bad?* Alex thought. *Are these orcs or the undead?*

The orcs continued past Alex and the rest of them. Apparently, orc eyes were just as bad as human eyes in the dark. They didn't take any notice of the gnome, drow, pixie, or human who were squashed against the wall, nor did they smell them.

Alex could see the outlines of the orcs through the gloom. She saw that they were holding very long, curved scimitars and had what looked like rifles across their backs. This surprised Alex, but she was growing used to weapons other than medieval fantasy warfare.

They were still a ways from the dragon stables, and if there were going to be this many orcs in the halls, it was going to be slow going. There had to be a faster way to get from point A to point B.

Unfortunately, it wasn't the best time to discuss that. The orcs were still lazily walking down the hall. It didn't seem as if they were in any rush. This made Alex wonder again what they were doing at the Nest.

If this had been as simple as "kill all the cadets," you would think the orcs would be acting with more urgency. The way they were slowly moving through the corridors didn't support that, though. So, what were they here for?

Once the orcs were out of earshot, Gill and Alex moved the group forward. Alex thought they needed to take a moment to regroup. Their initial plan was going to get much more complicated.

Alex guided the group to the mess hall. Gill checked to see if there were any orcs in the immediate vicinity, and Alex was certain that she couldn't smell any of them. All she could smell was the food in the hall.

They reached the door of the mess hall, and Alex extended her hand to open the door with the crystal datapad. When the five of them were inside the mess hall, Alex guided them to a table and sat down.

Brath looked around, trying to figure out where he was.

Manny'd had a harder time adjusting to the dark than he had been prepared for. "Is this the mess hall?" he asked. "By the realms, how were you ever able to see like this?"

Alex laughed despite herself and their current situation. "Trust me, it's not any easier if you've never seen anything before," she replied.

Jollies, who had been riding on Brath's shoulder, tried to flutter over to sit down on the table but got turned around and ended up on the floor. "Why did you bring us here?" Jollies asked.

"Because I realized there is a huge flaw in our plan," Alex

explained. "This place has got to be crawling with orcs. There's no way that we're going to be able to sneak past all of them to get to the stables."

"Wait, what do you mean?"

"I don't think the orcs are here just to attack the cadets. You know, if this was a raid, I'd be busting my ass to get to the end as soon as possible, especially if the raid was on a super-secret base with tons of dragons. But they're taking their time, almost like they know something we don't."

Brath reached out, trying to find the table, and tripped over his feet. He got up with Manny's help. "What do you think we should do?" he asked.

Gill pulled up his HUD visor, and it glowed dimly in the dark as he scrolled through it. "There are orcs all over the Nest, and they seem to have stopped attacking people. Most of the cadets are holed up on the other side. Guess it was just our hallway where the orcs were killing people."

For the first time since Alex had arrived at the Nest, she was glad she hadn't gotten to know anyone else. It would have killed her to have been close to any of the other cadets who got hurt. She knew everyone else must be hurting. She'd seen Jollies, Brath, and Gill with some of the kids on their floor.

If Gill was upset, he was hiding it very well. His voice was even and neutral, devoid of any emotion when he spoke. Alex wondered if that was a drow thing. "I don't think we should focus on rescuing anyone. The instructors are capable of that."

Jollies squeaked loudly, and her skin became brilliant red. "Wait, are you saying we should just leave them?"

Brath shook his head. "I'm saying we never planned to do any sort of rescue to begin with. And we are also unarmed unless you want to count my knife. The instructors must know what's going on. It would be stupid to try to do what they should be doing. We should stick to trying to get to our dragons."

There was a loud clatter of steel pots and pans in the mess hall, followed by shouts in orcish. All of the kids froze, staring at where they thought the noise had come from. There was someone else in the mess hall!

Gill grabbed Alex's hand and pointed in the direction of the orcs. He leaned over and whispered into Alex's ear, "There are two of them, smaller ones than the others. I can't tell what they're doing, though. I think they might just be eating. They might not know we're here."

Alex turned to Brath. "Give me your knife."

Brath gasped quietly. "Are you kidding me?" he asked. "No. It's my family's—"

"Here," Gill said, pulling a small curved dagger from his side. "I have two. What are you—"

Alex took the knife and pointed toward the orcs. "I'm going to take care of them."

Brath gulped. "We should run. Hide."

Gill pursed his lips before unsheathing his other knife. "No, she is right. This is our home, and it is under attack. We should do what we can. All right, Alex Bound, I shall follow you. I'll help. Brath, you coming?"

Brath shook his head. "I can't see well enough," he admitted. "But we'll stay here in case they slip past you. Maybe Jollies can light up the area enough to see if I need it." Alex noted that although there was fear in his voice, there was also disappointment. Brath was smart, and he wanted revenge on the Dark One more than anyone here. He would have come if he hadn't felt it was a suicide mission.

*Oh, God,* Alex thought. *I hope this isn't a suicide mission.*

Manny hovered in front of her. "You can't go. You'll get killed."

"Manny," Alex said, "I have to. Gill and I are the only ones who have a chance, and if we don't take them out, we'll all die. Let me do this. Please."

"And if you fail?"

"Then you, Brath, and Jollies haul ass and hide."

The Beholder considered for a moment before finally nodding. "Don't fail, then. Myrddin will kill me."

Alex touched the Beholder and nodded, then tugged Gill's hand. "Come on. You drows are supposed to be good at sneaking, right?"

Gill smiled, his sharp incisors glimmering in the darkness. "You could say that. Come on. We have to move fast."

There was another clatter and a sharp shout in Orcish.

Alex crouched, and Gill did the same. They slowly made their way toward the orcs, Gill occasionally stopping to point in the direction they needed to go. Alex's ears and nose were good, but Gill's darkvision was a godsend.

They were closing in on the orcs, who were now chattering loudly. She was right—whatever the orcs were planning, they were in no obvious rush.

As Alex and Gill got closer to the orcs, Alex's heart jumped up to her throat. What was she doing? She wasn't an assassin. She'd never even been in a real fight. How was she going to ambush two orcs and kill them?

This wasn't the time to be thinking like that, and Alex knew it. If she had thought like this during the joust, she would have lost. She didn't know if her instincts were any good, but all she could do was follow them. It was better than waiting to die.

Alex and Gill leaned against the wall. The orcs were in the back where the lunch folk usually cooked and passed out food. It seemed like they hadn't noticed the human and drow sneaking up on them.

Gill took Alex's hand and pointed to one of the orcs, then to himself, and then to the other orc. Simple enough. Alex was going to take the one on the right. Gill was going to take the one on the left.

Alex looked down at her knife. This was the first time she could remember ever holding a weapon, and she was going to use it to kill an orc. The thought made her stomach turn, but then she thought about the dead cadets she had seen in the hallway.

Alex squeezed Gill's hand and pointed forward. It was time. She crouched as low as she could to the floor, moving slowly, listening to the smacking lips of the orcs as they chewed on whatever food they had found.

From the corner of Alex's eye, she could see Gill's shape. He wasn't joking; he *was* good at sneaking. Alex pulled up the corner of her blindfold. She could hardly tell the drow from the shadows.

*God, that kid is hot,* she thought before remembering there was a full-grown orc ahead of her who was sorely in need of a knife in the back. *All right, I got this. I got this.* I got this!

Alex went forward, concentrating on making as little noise as she could. Gill was only a little way ahead of her.

The smell of the orcs was nearly overpowering. Alex thought Gill was lucky his sense of smell wasn't as good as hers. Both Alex and Gill reached the orcs. It was now or never.

Alex leaped onto the nearest orc's back and wrapped her hands around its throat. The orc screamed in shock as it tried to grab its sword.

Gill slashed at his orc's ankles, severing both of its Achilles tendons. The orc fell to the ground, screaming as it pulled out its rifle.

Alex squeezed her orc's throat as tightly as she could with one arm and raised her knife, then brought it down into the thing's neck. She couldn't believe how strong she was. There was something about being in Middang3ard; she was stronger than on Earth. Faster, too.

Like Captain America or Marvel, except without all the hand blaster stuff. God, that would have been cool.

The orc spun, its arms waving wildly as Alex stabbed it again and again, trying to keep from screaming as she hacked at its neck.

At her side, the surviving orc got hold of its rifle. It fired two shots that lit the room like a crack of lightning. In the brief period of light, Alex saw Gill's eyes flicker as he stepped into the shadows, his face covered in orc blood.

The orc turned to face Alex and aimed his rifle. Alex backed up, holding her knife in front of her, trying to figure out if she could close the gap between her and the orc before it fired. Then there was the sound of ripping flesh.

The orc fell with a knife in its back. Gill stepped forward, still hidden by the shadows, and grabbed his knife. "Don't forget yours."

Alex reached over to pick up the knife. Her hands were trembling, and she was struggling to breathe. She realized her shirt was covered with blood, and her face was wet and sticky with it. The acrid smell of copper filled her nostrils. "We...we did it," she mumbled.

Gill came over, grabbed Alex, and hugged her tight. "Your first one?" he asked.

Alex nodded as she hugged Gill back. He pulled away and held Alex's chin in his fingers. "If we don't kill them, they'll kill us. It's that simple. They will kill you, and they will not hesitate. Neither should you."

Alex wiped away a tear and smeared blood across her face. "Yeah, yeah. Come on."

"Hold on," Gill said as he leaned over the orc Alex had killed. "Take this."

Gill pulled the orc's head away from its body and tossed it

to Alex, who caught the head, surprised she hadn't jumped back in disgust. "This'll help get Brath off your back."

Alex leaned over and grabbed the orc's rifles. "And this is just being practical," she said.

"Good point. Let's see what else they have."

Alex and Gill looted the orcs' bodies and found three knives and two scimitars, but other than weapons, the orcs didn't have anything on them. Then they made their way back to Jollies, Manny, and Brath.

When Brath saw the two of them coming back, he shakily asked, "Is that you guys?"

Alex tossed the orc's head at Brath, who grabbed it out of the air before realizing what he had caught. He dropped the head and jumped back. "What the hell?" he yelped.

Gill came up beside Brath and handed him a sword. "That was Alex's," he explained. "Cut straight down to the bone. Nearly decapitated him."

Brath looked at Alex, his eyes wide and filled with awe. "Oh, that's… I mean, that's pretty cool," he said.

Alex tried not to look too smug and shrugged. "Just figured we needed to be able to catch our breath before we go back out there," she said. "And we can't do that with orcs snacking in here."

Manny rubbed his face with his tentacles. "What exactly were they snacking on in there?" he asked.

"Manny, this is not the time to be thinking about food!"

"Well, when is? I've been starving since we got kicked out of here."

Alex sighed as she realized Manny's body was probably burning more energy than usual since he was supporting both Brath and Jollies. "All right, go grab something to eat but hurry back," Alex said.

Manny didn't wait for Alex to say anything else. He rushed off, severing his ties with Jollies and Brath, who squeaked when their eyesight disappeared. Alex had completely forgotten how close Manny had to stay to keep the connection going. It looked like he had to stay even closer if he was running two at the same time.

Alex sat down next to Brath and took his trembling hand. "Hey, Jollies, could you get brighter for me?" Alex asked.

Jollies didn't answer but started to glow a deep blue as she fluttered over to Brath and Alex, who let go of Brath's hand. "Can you guys see all right?" Alex asked.

Jollies landed on Alex's knee. "How did you do this?" Jollies asked. "It's been fifteen minutes, and I already feel like I'm losing my mind. This was your entire life?"

"It's not that bad if it's all you've ever known. I never thought twice about it. I've heard of people losing their sight later in life, and that seems horrible. But this? It's all I ever knew."

Brath stared into the darkness. "Yeah, this is pretty hard. Must take a lot of guts to decide to jump on a dragon without even being able to see five feet in front of you."

"Makes it a lot harder when people are treating you like a lazy freak."

Brath didn't bother meeting Alex's eyes, but he nodded to show he understood what she was saying. "Yes, it would. So, what's the game plan?"

Alex wasn't expecting an apology from Brath, just an acknowledgment and she had gotten that. They could worry about their squabbles later. For now, they had to figure out how they were going to make it to the dragon stables with a Wasp's Nest full of orcs.

Manny came floating back toward the group, quietly munching on whatever grub he'd found. "We could take the service tunnels," Manny suggested. "They're not quite tunnels, more like invisible hallways. It's what all the extra regular staff use."

"Extra regular?"

"Like the cooks, cleaners, things like that—the staff who don't interact with students all the time. Can you imagine how annoyed the lunch lady would be if people tried to talk to her about lunch when she wasn't working behind the line? She's already pretty irritable."

Gill pulled up his HUD and looked through the schematics of the Wasp's Nest. "How do we get to them?" he asked.

"There should be an entrance somewhere in the back of the kitchen. We should be able to follow them all the way to the stables."

Alex stood up, sheathed her knife, and slung the rifle over her shoulder. "All right, what are we wasting time for then? Let's get going."

# CHAPTER THREE

Alex and the group made their way to the back of the kitchen. They had to tell Manny to stop grabbing more food, but the harder they tried to stop the Beholder, the more they found themselves grabbing food.

Stress was making everyone hungry.

Alex had only just stopped shaking since her encounter with the orc. She had managed to put up a brave front for Brath, but now she was replaying the whole scene in her head.

Alex was glad she had had her eyes covered. She didn't want to imagine what the gory mess would have looked like if she could have seen normally.

They were all crouched around an overturned platter of mashed potatoes and another food with a similar texture but wildly different in taste. Once everyone had had their fill, they got up and continued toward the back.

Manny stopped the group and motioned toward a door with his eye tentacles. "This would be it."

Gill walked up to the freezer and gave it a once-over. "Isn't this just a freezer?"

Manny shook his head, his tentacles swaying. "Only to the uninitiated. Most of the entry areas are disguised so cadets won't waste their time trying to get in. We were using broom closets for a while, but instructors quickly found out what teenagers use closets for."

Manny opened the freezer. Past the threshold was a portal that breathed cold, fresh air out at Alex and the rest of them. Even if she had been able to see, she probably would have assumed this was a freezer. "All right, let's go."

Alex and Gill went first since they were the ones who could see best. They stepped through the portal, which was unlike the first portal Myrddin had sent her through. There was no disorientation or anything like that. She merely walked through it and was somewhere else.

The somewhere else was a long hall much different from the glass corridors of the Wasp's Nest. These halls were bare and not crystalline. They looked as if they were made of simple wood and stone. "What's with the lack of magic?" Alex asked as she peeked through her blindfold.

As they walked, Manny explained the reason. "These are meant for quick transit. The whole Nest uses a large amount of energy. When they were putting these halls together, they figured just building them would be an easy way to keep from wasting energy."

Gill ran his hands across the walls, collecting cobwebs. "And no one ever made a plan for using these in case of an evacuation?"

"If I'm honest, Myrddin isn't the humblest man in the realms. He never thought anyone would have the gall to attack the Nest. And as we've seen tonight, that meant we were not running tight enough security."

Brath tapped his knife on his dragon anchor. "I'll say." He chuckled. "You'd think the place Myrddin spends most of his time would be better defended. Doesn't look good for the Resistance, does it?"

Alex turned to Brath despite not being able to see. "Wait, are you saying Myrddin is here?"

"I mean, he might not be here right now, but he usually is. From what I've heard, the dragonriders are his pet project, after the MERCs."

"Well, why doesn't he just blast these orcs out of here and stop all of this?"

"Beats me. Trust me; I wish he would too. Walking around in the magical back alleys of the Nest with a bunch of kids isn't my idea of a good time."

Alex almost regretted having engaged Brath, but he was right. It wasn't a particularly great idea, and it also didn't do much to make her trust Myrddin's foresight. Why would he have left this place so poorly defended?

Gill pulled up his visor HUD and scrolled through a map, trying to find out where they were in the Nest. "Come on, guys, talking trash on Myrddin right now isn't going to help any of us. Let's just focus on what we can control. We follow this for a while, then turn right and hit the stables."

Alex and the rest of them moved through the dark hallway in silence. It was welcome since Alex was finally able to be alone with her thoughts. She had been trying to roll with the punches since the invasion. Truthfully, since she had arrived at the Nest. It wasn't getting any easier.

Myrddin had made it seem like she would be safe—as if her mother and father didn't have anything to worry about. Alex had been at the Nest for less than a week, and she was already fleeing for her life, with Myrddin nowhere to be seen.

*Crap*, Alex thought. *Did my parents respond?*

Alex opened her HUD and checked for messages. Her parents had responded almost instantly. This wasn't the time to answer, but Alex promised herself she was going to make it through this if only to speak to her parents again.

Gill raised his hand to signal to the group to stop. "Wait. I see heat signatures up ahead through the walls. I want to check and see what they are." Gill looked down at his map. "Oh, no. Those are cadets. They're hiding. They're not too far from here."

Alex didn't wait for him to say anything more. "We have to go help them. We can't just leave them there by themselves."

Brath forced his way up from the back of the group. "Weren't you the ones who were saying we had to focus on getting to our dragons and that it was the *adults'* job to figure out how to save the cadets?"

"Yeah, but that was before they were only a couple of feet away from us," Gill countered. "I thought it was stupid to try to fight our way through half of the Nest to get to them, but these guys are right here. It's a considerably smaller risk."

Sometimes Alex hated the way Gill talked. He sounded like a walking computer program. She wondered if he was even capable of feeling anything. The way he had handled killing that orc was positively cold, even though he had been right.

Jollies shimmered from pink to red as she flew up to Alex's face. "We can't leave them behind," she pleaded.

Alex swiped her finger across Jollies' face. "Dude, don't even worry about it. That was never an option. We're supposed to be training to be heroes, aren't we? Might as well start now. Take us there, Gill."

Gill nodded as he turned his attention back to his map. There was a little bit more light in the hall, so it was easier to move around. They must have been off the main power grid of the Nest. Alex wondered if that meant they were more protected or less.

It didn't take long to find where the cadets were being held. Gill looked through his map one more time and cross-referenced the surveillance videos. As it turned out, the cadets weren't hiding. They had been captured by orcs patrolling the area.

Gill pulled up a couple of videos that had been taken before the power shut off. It looked like the orcs were regularly patrolling the area, making sure no one came for the cadets. "Great, this just went from stupid to impossible," Brath grumbled.

"Are there any breaks in their pattern?" Alex asked. "Or are they just checking in every couple of minutes?'

Gill scrolled past a few videos. "It doesn't look like there's a pattern," he admitted. "I think they just come in when they want. They aren't even checking up that often."

"So, all we gotta do is slip in and out fast. Real sneaky-like. Sounds easy enough."

Gill chuckled softly, the sound reverberating in the silence of the corridor. "You know, you're a little reckless."

"Yeah, just a little."

# CHAPTER FOUR

The cadet dragonriders pressed their ears to the walls, hoping the walls were thin enough to hear through. Gill had brought them to where he said the other cadets were being held. Alex couldn't hear anything. The walls weren't as thin as she had hoped.

Gill looked at his map one more time, checking to see if there were any orcs patrolling the area. It looked clear. "Where will we take them?" Gill suddenly asked, realizing there was a massive gap in their plan.

Alex wracked her brain, trying to think of a place the other cadets might be safe. "Uh, I guess we'll just bring them with us," she finally said. "They're all cadets too. That means they're probably bound to dragons as well. More fighters for the battle."

Gill's eyes went wide. "Wait, you didn't say anything about a battle!"

Alex turned to face the drow. "What did you think we were going to get our dragons for? To run away? We can't leave everyone here without helping."

Gill nodded that he understood before looking back

down at his map. "It's just that you weren't specific about wanting to fight."

An arm broke through the wall and wrapped itself around Alex's throat. Alex let out a sharp yelp as she was pulled through the wall by the muscular gray arm of an orc.

The orc tossed Alex across the room, and she hit the opposite wall with a heavy thud. She would have assumed the force of the impact would knock her out. It didn't and Alex, surprised, got to her feet. Her back still hurt like hell, though. "Huh, that's new," she muttered.

There wasn't any time to revel in her realization because the orc who had grabbed her was running toward her.

The cadets in the room started screaming and asking for help as Alex tried to get her bearings.

The room was still pitch-black. Even though the orc had managed to snag her through the wall, it didn't seem to be able to find her in the dark room. The place was larger than Alex had assumed, based on the map Gill had shown her.

That was when Alex remembered the Nest was plugged into everyone who was residing within it—everyone other than the invaders. The room had probably expanded based on Alex's need, and she needed a very large room at the moment.

Alex turned and ran as she shouted, "Jollies, find me. I have an idea!" She knew she was going to give away her position, but it was more important that Jollies know where she was. If Jollies came for her, the rest of them would as well. Then they'd have a chance against the orc.

Alex wasn't sure she could take the orc by herself. She preferred not to think about it chasing after her, gnashing its teeth and waiting to sink its blade into her chest. She had managed to kill one before, and it hadn't been too hard.

*There's no way I could have done that back on Earth,* Alex thought as she realized she wasn't having any trouble breathing. She hadn't been unfit before, but physical education wasn't her strong suit.

It seemed like Alex's body had been given an upgrade since she had arrived at the Wasp's Nest. Maybe her Captain America theory wasn't wrong after all.

She wasn't sure if it was the realm she was in (honestly, she was still confused as to exactly where the Nest was) or if it was her armor.

Suddenly, the prospect of fighting an orc didn't seem as terrible. Maybe she wasn't as weak and defenseless as she'd thought. Maybe she was just scared, and being scared was something she could deal with.

Alex ran straight ahead, hoping she wasn't going to run into a wall, but the wall never came. She could still hear the orc behind her.

It was time for the first step of the plan. Alex stopped, turned around, and sprinted straight back the way she had come.

As Alex ran, she could hear the orc getting closer, but it was somewhere to the side. She had figured the orc was going to be searching, walking back and forth, unaware of exactly where Alex was.

It didn't take long to sprint past the orc and around the corner.

Now was the hard part. Alex stopped running and pulled up her blindfold a little bit. She could see the faint outlines of her friends in the darkness, and she ran toward them. "Jollies!" she whispered as loud as she could.

It was enough for Jollies to hear. The pixie came racing over to Alex. "There you are," she exclaimed. "Where are the other—"

"We're going to worry about them in a second. We have to deal with that orc before he catches us again. Can you control your colors?"

"Yeah, if I try hard."

"Can you make them brighter?"

"I might be able to."

That was enough for Alex. It was going to be a gamble, but Alex realized she was comfortable taking risks in these kinds of situations. "All right, come with me. Gill and Brath, can you stay with Manny and start helping the cadets?"

Brath stepped forward and pulled out his dagger. "Don't you want backup?" he asked.

"I'd love some, but more people with me means fewer people to help the cadets. Also, that would put three of us in danger for a really stupid plan I'm still not sure is going to work. Sorry, Jollies."

Gill rested his hand on Brath's shoulder and turned the gnome around. "Come on, we need to help the other cadets."

Brath, Gill, and Manny went back in the direction they thought the other cadets might be in. In the dark distance, there was a roar from the orc.

Alex reached out to Jollies. "Could I hold you?" she asked. "It'll make moving in the dark easier since you're going to be farther from Manny."

Jollies flew into Alex's palm, and she closed it as loosely as she could to keep from hurting Jollies. Then she took off in the direction of the orc's shout. "All right, Jollies," Alex explained. "On my signal, you're going to turn bright white, okay?"

Alex could feel Jollies nodding. Then Alex stopped for a second, trying to calm her heart so she could listen for the footsteps of the orc. It was going to be a race to see who heard the other first. Alex had a slight upper hand, or at least she thought she did. She wasn't sure if orcs had better vision in the dark.

The orc grunted, voicing his frustration at his prey getting away. That was all Alex needed. She sprinted toward the sound. When she thought she was close enough, she squeezed Jollies a little bit.

Jollies got the point, shut her eyes, and tensed her whole body until she flashed bright white. The part of the room they were in brightened instantly.

The orc turned around, dazed and confused, his eyes trying to adjust to the sudden bright light. Alex pulled out her knife and slammed it into his chest, pushing him back against the wall.

The orc didn't go down. It wrapped its hands around Alex's neck and lifted her into the air.

Alex gasped for air as she pulled out her knife and drove it into the orc's skull. It let go of her and fell to the ground dead as Jollies' white light faded.

Jollies flew down to the orc to check if it was really dead. "Holy crap," Jollies gasped. "That just happened. You killed him!"

Alex wiped the blood off her blade before she sheathed it. She was still trying to catch her breath, but her neck didn't hurt as much as she expected.

Her second orc of the day.

Alex knelt beside the body of the orc and checked it for anything useful, but found nothing. *Guess this place is not going to beat that VR randomly-generated loot system.* She laughed.

The limits of Alex's physical body had definitely been extended. She was strong enough to drive a knife through solid bone. That was definitely an upgrade.

Jollies perched atop Alex's shoulder. "That was crazy. I didn't know you were such a tough guy. Never would have thought it from how you were acting with Brath."

Alex chuckled as she walked back toward where she thought the other cadets were. "Well, I wasn't trying to kill

Brath. Dealing with bullies is harder than killing an orc. At least the orcs aren't trying to torture me psychologically."

By the time Alex and Jollies caught up with the other cadets, Brath and Gill had freed them all. "You took care of the orc?" Brath asked.

Jollies lit up bright white for a second, illuminating everyone. "Oh, man, you should have seen it! She was so flippin' cool! That orc didn't stand a chance."

At least ten other cadets had been captured. Alex could barely make them out in the dark. She didn't want to waste time trying to introduce herself to everyone, so she just asked the group, "How are you guys? Is everyone okay?"

A quiet voice came from the mass of bodies. "Yeah, they didn't do anything to us. They just said they were going to hold onto us for someone."

"For someone?"

"Yeah, they kept going on like they were waiting for someone."

Alex looked around the room, trying to make out its features and figure out where exactly in the Nest they were. "Uh, anyone know where we are?" she asked.

Gill pulled up his map and pointed to its center. "We're in the Great Hall. Guess when we aren't all paying attention, the Nest relaxes or something."

"Is this place alive?"

"Honestly, I'm starting to wonder about that."

Suddenly, there was a bright flash of light. Alex was dazed for a second and she covered her eyes, but before she could orient herself, a strong force like a wall of metal slammed against her and sent her flying.

Alex struggled to get to her feet as her eyes adjusted to the light.

"Ah," a deep voice crooned. "More cadets for me."

# CHAPTER FIVE

In the blinding light of the Great Hall stood a man in a black cloak, its hood pulled down over his face. The light was emanating from him. He held a gnarled wooden staff with a glowing crystal atop it.

The man pulled back his hood. It was impossible to tell if he was an elf or a human or some other race. The features of his face seemed to shift continually, his eyebrows growing larger and moving as his eyes dropped to his mouth, which curled up to his ears.

The dark wizard raised his staff and laughed, a sickening sound like glass being broken. "I am Holmorth for the Dark One, and I have come for you, dragonriders!" the creature screeched, his high-pitched voice making Alex's ears prickle. "*My* dragonriders!"

A horde of orcs filled the hall behind Holmorth. They looked like a pack of rabid dogs waiting for their master to unleash them.

Alex pulled her blindfold back down as she made her way to her feet. It was too bright, and there was too much visual information for her to process. She was glad to cover her eyes again. The image of Holmorth's contorting face would probably haunt her nightmares. Seeing it once was enough.

Manny severed his psychic ties with the cadets and floated ahead of them. This action forced Alex to use her own eyes.

The Beholder squared off against Holmorth, all of his eyes facing forward, giving the wizard his undivided attention. "Holmorth, what are you doing here?" he asked. "Have you gotten bored pretending to be a dark magician in that hell pit you call a home?"

Holmorth laughed again and swiped his staff upward. A bolt of lightning issued from it and hit the ceiling, sending a cascade of glass falling. The recently rescued cadets screamed in fear as they backed up, inching closer to the far edge of the hall.

Alex, Brath, Jollies, and Gill did not retreat. They held their ground behind Manny, who had moved forward, his eyes still trained on Holmorth.

Holmorth rested his staff against his shoulder as he chuckled. "I see Myrddin is still having you play babysitter," he said tauntingly. "I wonder why a powerful and eldritch creature such as you has allowed a lowly human to make you his errand boy?"

Manny's body swelled as if he were growing in size. A pulse of energy came off him, which Alex felt wash over her like a wave of heat. "We both know Myrddin is far from being a lowly human," the Beholder countered. "He's a finer wizard than you'll ever be. I'd be surprised if you are even capable of handling me alone."

Another wave of energy came off Manny, hotter than the last. "Apparently you need an entire army to deal with children now," he followed up. "Are your powers waning? So sad to see your potential wasted."

Holmorth took a step forward, and dark energy radiated

from his body. Even though the light was shining from him, he was still cloaked in blackness. "Hardly," Holmorth said, snarling. "Nothing you taught me has been wasted, unlike that fool Myrddin."

Holmorth waved his hand, and the floor before him broke into spikes that floated into the air and flew at Manny.

Manny did nothing, yet when the spikes should have hit him, they disintegrated into pebbles.

Holmorth laughed again, the same ear-piercing sound. "You are wasting *your* potential, Manny. The Dark One would reward power such as yours instead of delegating his menial tasks to you. An eldritch being of your power should be a ruler."

"And that's what you're doing? The Dark One wants to rule. He won't share it with anyone."

"That is where you are wrong, Manny. The Dark One will indeed rule, and there are some of us who will also rule what has been given to us through his many graces."

One of Manny's eyes flipped over and looked at Alex before he turned to face the cadets. "Do you all have weapons?" he asked.

Alex and the rest of them solemnly nodded, and Jollies pulled a tiny crossbow out of her knapsack. Alex whispered to the Beholder, "If you could do all that, why not save us all the stress? The cards, the sneaking around. You could have just blasted them the whole time."

"Because I won't always be with you, and I needed you to see your actions and understand your potential. You are a leader who cares for her soldiers. You are a strategist who seeks survival over frivolous battle, and you are more powerful than you know. Myrddin was right about you, Alex the Boundless. I am proud to have been your eyes, as brief as that time has been." the Beholder's eyes softened as he looked upon her. Then turning to everyone, he said in a loud voice,

"Good that you have weapons, because you're going to have to fight your way to the stables. I'll hold them off for as long as I can, but you make it to the stables and you leave. Don't turn back. Don't try to help anyone else. Do you understand me?"

Alex grabbed the rifle slung over her shoulder. "No way," she shouted. "We're not just going to leave you."

"You have to. You cadets are more important than me. You're the hope of Middang3ard. Do you understand me?"

A bolt of plasma went flying past Manny and hit an orc in the chest. The rest of the orcs screamed, ready to bolt forward, but Holmorth held his hand up to keep them back.

Gill, who was holding his smoking rifle, shrugged. "We'll go," he said slowly. "But we aren't leaving you alone. If we're running, so are you."

Manny sighed as one of his eyes flipped over to watch the horde of orcs across the room. "Fine, we'll all go," he agreed. "But I'm going to need to stall Holmorth if we're going to make it. When I say go, go. No questions asked. Understood?"

Manny faced Holmorth again and floated forward as the dark wizard started to walk toward Manny. "I assume you still honor the old ways?" the Beholder asked. "The eldritch traditions I trained you in?"

Holmorth folded his arms and snarled, then he nodded.

Manny and Holmorth stood face to face a few feet from each other. "Good. Shall we begin?"

Holmorth said nothing, only clutched his staff. He aimed it at Manny, and a bolt of lightning fired from it.

Manny raised one of his eyes, and the lightning deflected and struck the wall. Then Manny's eyes burned bright white, and a black hand, twice as large as Holmorth, appeared in the air. The hand grabbed Holmorth and wrung him as if he were a wet towel.

Holmorth shouted, and the boom of his voice destroyed the hand. He fell to the ground and grabbed his staff, then turned and aimed it at one of the orcs.

The orc was hit with a blast of green light, and it fell over as its body started to swell and bulge. A tentacle ripped out of it—a creature was growing within it. Within seconds, a massive kraken burst from the orc's body.

The kraken flew at Manny, who floated to the side as quickly as he could. The kraken was easily the size of a bus, its tentacles flying about as it screeched, clacking its beak.

Alex raised her rifle and took aim at the kraken.

One of Manny's eyes flipped over and saw Alex. "No!" he shouted. "Don't interfere. This is between Holmorth and me!"

The kraken reared its head as Holmorth aimed his staff at Manny, shooting a fireball that went careening toward the Beholder.

Manny dodged the fireball and turned his attention to the kraken. Manny's eyes shifted color again, glowing bright white.

The walls next to the kraken shot out spikes, impaling it.

One of Manny's tentacles sketched a shape, an ancient sigil from times long past. The kraken's skin caught fire and it burned to nothing but bone and ash. Then the ash rose from the ground.

Manny turned to face Holmorth. He pointed one of his eyes at the black wizard and the ash from the kraken flew toward Holmorth, covering his body in black soot.

Holmorth struggled and tried to escape but could do nothing.

Manny retreated back toward the cadets and shouted, "Now! Let's go!"

The cadets broke into a run toward the back of the Great Hall as Holmorth tried to free himself. The black wizard screamed in rage and then shouted, "Don't just stand there, you idiots! Kill them! Kill them all!"

The orcs ran toward the cadets, who had already made it to the end of the hall. The crystal door presented a datapad, and Manny slammed his tentacle onto it, shouting, "Open faster, damn you!"

The crystal doors opened, and the cadets rushed through. The doors shut quickly behind them and Manny commanded the doors to lock before heading toward the stables.

The orcs could be heard firing their plasma rifles from behind the door, trying to break through.

Alex was running beside Manny. "Damn, dude, that was really impressive," she said. "I didn't know you were that strong."

Manny chuckled before coughing and wheezing, trying to catch his breath. "It's been a while since I've had a duel of thoughts," he admitted. "Honestly, I didn't know how well I was going to do. I'm glad I made it out alive. I didn't go into recruitment to have fights like that."

Alex thought back to all the time Manny had spent helping her without saying anything. Having seen how powerful he was, she knew he could be using his talents anywhere else. It meant a lot to her that he had stuck by her for so long.

The cadets took a right turn at a corner and continued running. Behind them, Alex heard the door Manny had locked explode. Holmorth's scream echoed down the hall.

The most frantic cadets were toward the front of the group, mostly younger students. Many of them were crying. Alex wouldn't have been surprised if they were imagining how they were going to die. She might have been doing the same if it had been earlier in the day. Now all she could think about was getting to Chine.

Alex reached out to her dragon with her mind. She wasn't sure if she was close enough to speak to him. Even though she had been fairly certain she could navigate the Wasp's Nest blind, running through hallway after hallway while being chased by orcs had left her a little disoriented.

There was no reply. Alex tried again, focusing as hard as she could manage on Chine. *Hey, Chine! Are you okay?* she sent.

Still no reply. For the first time since the invasion started, Alex worried if Chine was alive. She had to get to him as fast as possible. If anything happened to him... Well, Alex didn't know, but she felt the consequences would be terrible.

# CHAPTER SIX

The cadets raced down the changing halls of the crystal Nest. Alex had assumed the path would be straightforward, as it always had been before, but the Wasp's Nest was doing its job. The nest was providing the cadets with what they needed: confusion to their enemies.

As the party ran through the hall, everyone trying to get their bearings, Gill shouted left or right as he saw fit. Alex could hear the orcs chasing them, their roars making them seem like a horde of nightmares eager for a butchering.

Gill was at the head of the group of cadets. He was doing a great job of keeping a level head, but Alex doubted he was ever anything other than calm. Regardless of the Nest trying to keep the orcs away from the cadets, Gill was making sense out of the ever-changing labyrinth.

Jollies had decided it made more sense to rest in Alex's hand. She wasn't used to flying so strenuously, and she was exhausted.

Brath, on the other hand, was up front with Gill, occasionally shouting to the cadets to keep going, rallying them.

Manny stayed at the back in case any of the orcs or Holmorth started to close in on the cadets.

Alex was replaying Manny's battle with Holmorth in her head. She had never seen magic used in battle before. Not like that, at least. She had seen the Nest, and that was very different. Panic was starting to creep up on her, but she shoved it down as far as she could.

*This isn't the time to freak out,* Alex thought. *I keep telling myself that. When is the time to freak out? Freaking out would feel kind of nice about now.*

For some reason, Alex had become extremely worried about Chine. She couldn't get him out of her mind, and it confused her.

Gill pointed ahead and shouted, "Left now!"

The cadets took the left and the Nest closed the hallway behind them. They stood before a large crystal double door —the stables, at last.

One of the cadets reached out to the datapad next to the door. She pressed her hand to it, and the doors swung open. The cadets rushed in.

Manny turned to Gill and told him to turn the lights back on. It didn't make sense to be running around in the dark. They might as well be able to see everything.

Gill did as he was told, hacking into the system as quickly as he could. The lights flickered on after a couple of seconds. Without thinking, Alex pulled off her blindfold. The light flooded her eyes, but she pushed past the pain.

The room was blurry but quickly coming into focus. Once her eyesight returned to her, she wished she could have looked away.

The stables were almost completely destroyed. There was rubble everywhere and no dragons to be seen. Alex thought back to the tremors and explosions she had felt when the invasion had first started. She hadn't seen any damage to the rest of the Nest. The attack must have been focused on the dragon stables.

Alex grabbed Manny and shouted, "I need to find Chine!"

Manny avoided Alex's eyes. He floated away, trying to get a grasp of just how much damage was done. "They can't be dead," Manny whispered. "Their cadets would have felt it. Everyone would have felt it."

Brath walked away from the other cadets and said, "Maybe the Nest helped them like it's been helping us. They could be hiding."

Alex needed that little bit of hope. Hope was all she had. She pushed her way through the rest of the stunned cadets and ran farther into the main area, looking around to see if she could find where the dragons might have gone.

It felt like Alex's whole plan was falling apart. She had put everyone in danger in the hope of getting to their dragons. Now they might be gone.

*Everyone could end up dead because of me,* she thought.

Her chest closed up, and her heart was racing. She kept thinking of the orcs—their footsteps echoing in the hall, their screams as they readied their swords and rifles. It was almost too much.

Tears poured out of the rider's eyes. She felt like her heart was curling up. She wanted to scream, to cry, to be anywhere but where she was right then, yet she was there. The orcs weren't going anywhere, and neither was she.

Alex faced the rest of the cadets. She didn't bother wiping the tears from her face. Instead, she stared at the cadets as she hiccupped through her tears. "Manny says the dragons are here," she said, her voice more confident than she felt. "Everyone, find your dragon. This is where we fight."

Alex stepped away from the cadets, unsure if she had just ordered everyone to their deaths. It didn't matter, though.

Death had come for them. It was time to find out if they could postpone it for a little longer.

The cadets split up. No one said a word. They were all driven by the urge to find their dragons. Alex thought it might have to do with the binding. Maybe it was more than just the words Myrddin had said. The binding was obviously something far beyond Alex's understanding.

Alex forced herself to stop thinking. She shoved away every thought that crept into her mind. There was only one thing to focus on—finding Chine. She reached out again, shouting in her mind, *Chine! Where are you? Chine!*

Chine's voice came screaming through Alex's head. She nearly fell over from the force of his thoughts. *Child of Dust!* Chine shouted. *I have been trying to find you for hours. Are you okay? Please tell me you're well?*

Alex stopped running and stood still. Chine had been worried about her. He had known something was going wrong. And he was alive. Most importantly, he was alive. *I'm okay*, Alex thought to him. *The Nest is under attack. Where are you?*

*We're hidden. Some kind of magic of the Nest. You can turn it off. Find the central switch. Release us.* There was fire in Chine's thoughts. The dragon wanted to fight.

Alex scanned the stables, trying to see where the central control system was. Everything was rubble. It was impossible to see anything. *It's not impossible,* Alex thought. *I can do this. I can do this.*

An explosion rocked the stables. Alex and the other cadets who were searching for their dragons turned to the doors of the stables.

Holmorth stood on the threshold, his staff raised, the orcs at his back. "Kill them!" Holmorth shouted.

The orcs poured into the room as the cadets shrieked and sprinted off. If she left the cadets, they were all going to die.

Manny went flying toward the orcs, his eyes white and filled with fury. The walls of the Nest bent to his will and shards of crystal flew, impaling six orcs and nailing them to the wall.

Behind Manny, Gill and Brath pulled out their rifles and fired at every orc they could see.

An orc slipped past the plasma fire and grabbed Brath by his red cap. The gnome screamed and fired a bolt of hot plasma point-blank that ripped through the orc's face.

Manny was floating in the air, all of his tentacles flailing wildly. A concussive force shot out of him, pushing all of the orcs and Holmorth back toward the doors.

Alex started to work her way through the rubble. She had no idea what the control system looked like. She had never seen it through Manny's eyes and had never touched it. This was worse than looking for a needle in a haystack. At least most people know what a needle and a haystack looked like.

Alex ran through the throng of cadets who were dispersing through the room as Manny continued to push the orcs and Holmorth back. Brath and Gill, now at his side, were shooting any orcs who managed to get past Manny's psychic powers.

As Alex was running, her foot hit a large stone. She toppled over and fell into a pile of crystals and computer parts. When she sat up, she saw a computer screen. *Could this be it?* Alex thought. She scrambled to the computer screen and tried to find the keyboard. It was shattered, along with the CPU.

There wasn't time to be concerned with what else was going around her. The dragon stables were filled with the scent of hot plasma and the screams of cadets and orcs. To look at it would have been too much. The only thing Alex could do was find the central computer switch. That was the important thing.

Alex picked herself up from the rubble and continued to search, grabbing anything in the crystal and dust that looked like it could help. Her mind was racing. Every possible scenario of her death played out in her head, but she kept searching.

"What are you doing in my stables!" a voice shouted over the cacophony.

Alex looked over her shoulder toward the source of the voice.

Tribble and Primerose were at another door in the stables. Primerose was carrying a gun or sword in each of her hands, reminding Alex of the god Kali. Tribble held two plasma machine guns, the straps over her shoulders. "These are *my* stables!" Tribble shouted as she started firing.

Primerose leaped at the orcs in front of her. Her hands were moving faster than Alex could see, slashing at orcs and firing at the same time.

Alex made herself look away. She was overwhelmed by all she was seeing. She had to focus. She had to find Chine and the other dragons. Alex pulled herself to her feet and ran through the stables, stopping to check any computer she saw.

A green switch, set apart from the rest of the tech around, sat in a pile of crystal dust. Alex saw it, ran toward it, and scooped it up in her hand. *Please let this be it,* she thought before flipping the switch.

There was a rush of air. Alex looked around. The Nest was gone. She was standing in a field of flowers. A blue sky filled with clouds was overhead. *You found me,* a familiar voice said.

Alex spun around and saw Chine sitting comfortably in the field. *Where are we?* Alex asked. *Why aren't you helping us?*

Chine stood and shook himself, his scales rising as if he was a cat. *We were put here,* he explained. *As soon as the attack happened. But you can bring us out.*

*How?*

Chine pointed upward. Alex stared up at a portal in the sky. *Through there. I'll follow, and the rest will as well. Are you ready?*

Alex hardly heard what Chine was saying. She leaped and landed on Chine's back, then raised her dragon anchor and felt it connect. "Let's do this!" she shouted.

Chine roared loudly as Alex pulled back on her anchor and leaned forward, urging Chine toward the portal.

The two of them passed through the portal and came out in the Wasp's Nest. Manny was still holding off as many of the orcs as he could.

Holmorth had forced his way to the front of the fight. Lightning and fire shot from his staff as he pushed to get closer to Manny.

Chine landed in front of Manny and shot a jet of ether fire toward Holmorth.

The wizard pulled his staff back and covered his face, casting a barrier around himself that split the black fire around him. It engulfed the orcs who surrounded him.

Alex pulled her rifle from her back and started firing. The closest orcs fell.

Chine shot another plume of ether fire at the orcs surrounding him as Holmorth raised his staff, speaking in the old infernal tongue, preparing to conjure a creature.

Manny screamed, "Alex, don't let him finish!"

Alex leaned forward, pulling her dragon anchor toward her. Chine charged toward Holmorth. That was when Alex understood the binding. What had taken place between her and Chine did not exist in a place of words, sight, or anything else. They were connected.

As Holmorth raised his staff to cast his spell, Chine grabbed the wizard. Alex could feel the adrenaline racing through the dragon's body.

The dragon chomped down hard, trying to separate Holmorth's body and seeking to swallow the top half. Before he could, the wizard disappeared, evidently choosing retreat over death.

The orcs were still screeching, firing their plasma rifles as dragon after dragon poured from the portal at the top half of the stables. The dragons found their way to their riders, each rider leaping atop their dragon.

It did not take long for the stables to be full of fire, lightning, and ice. The cadets did what they had been trained to do, each of them falling into their own pattern.

Alex flew above them all, watching the dragonriders drive off the orcs, burning or skewering any who were not wise enough to flee.

As Alex and Chine were flying, the doors of the stables burst open. A dragon ripped through the crystal, but it was not like any dragon Alex had seen before. It was a mech, yet almost indiscernible from the real thing.

The chest of the mech dragon opened, and Roy leaned out. His face was covered in blood and he shouted, "We rally here! If it's an orc, it dies!"

Roy's mech rampaged through the orcs in front of it, tearing them apart as its fire engulfed the rest. The dragonrider cadets followed Roy's order and converged on the orcs.

The orcs fired plasma rifle blasts, but it was not enough. They fell. The dragonriders had won.

# CHAPTER SEVEN

The funeral started around noon.

It had only been a day since the invasion. Nothing felt normal, if it had felt normal to begin with. Once the last of the orcs had been cleaned up, the remaining instructors and Myrddin had ushered everyone back to their rooms. No one had wanted to talk about anything.

Alex had spent the night staring at the ceiling of her room. She had spent countless nights in her life staring at her ceiling but had never actually seen it. The darkness she had known before would have been preferable.

Sometime during the night, as she was struggling to sleep, she opened the message she had received from her parents.

It was a video of them sitting next to each other, encouraging her to quit trying to fit in with everyone. They said that if people were worthy of her time, they would make themselves evident.

Alex almost laughed when she saw the message. The whole situation seemed so hard for her to understand now. She wasn't concerned with a gnome picking on her, not anymore. There were orcs who wanted her dead, an army at the Dark One's orders. What were bullies compared to that?

For a moment, Alex thought about sending her parents a message to let them know what had happened over the last twenty-four hours. She thought more about it and decided it wasn't a good idea. Even she didn't quite understand what had happened over the last day.

There had been lunch, a joust, and then an invasion by orcs and a dark wizard. That wasn't something you sent in a casual message.

Instead, Alex pulled up her HUD visor and said, "Hey, Mom! Hey, Dad! I just got your message. Things have been going a lot better. That bully I was talking about? We're not friends, but we also don't hate each other anymore. And I have a really cool roommate. Also, there's a hot dark elf. Hope everything is going well. I love and miss you guys."

Alex ended the recording and sent the message. That was probably the most her parents were going to be able to deal with. She did say there was a hot elf.

Next was getting out of bed and getting ready for the funeral, the real part of the day. Jollies still hadn't come back from breakfast so Alex had the room all to herself. It didn't matter, though. She didn't feel like enjoying her solitude.

The door opened, and Jollies fluttered into the room. She went straight to her bed and laid down. "Hey, dude, everything okay?" Alex asked.

Jollies rolled over and said, "Breakfast was hard. There were a lot of people missing."

That was one of the reasons Alex hadn't wanted to go to breakfast. She didn't want to know the extent of how many cadets had been lost during the battle. It was ultimately unavoidable, but seeing it would hurt.

Jollies sat up and wiped tears from her eyes. "Almost time to get going, right?" she asked.

Alex came over to Jollies' bed and rested her hand next to it, palm open, for the pixie to climb onto if she wanted. "Yeah, it's getting to be about that time."

The funeral took place in the Great Hall. The Wasp's Nest had repaired itself, and It looked like nothing had happened. But the cadets knew.

Caskets were lined up before a podium, each of them open, each of them honored.

Myrddin stood behind the podium, his face grim and settled. The rest of the instructors sat behind him, all of them wearing black. Toppinir and Roy sat close to Myrddin, looking uncomfortable.

Alex filed into the hall with the rest of the cadets, trying to ignore how few there were now. She remembered it had almost been impossible to count how many cadets there were in the mess hall. Now she could put them all in her dorm room.

It felt like a defeat to see how many cadets she hadn't saved. The hall felt bare, empty of souls.

At the front of the hall, Myrddin stood. He cleared his throat, and when he spoke, his voice was magically amplified to a soft boom, a resting thunder in the ears of the attendees. "Today we are gathered to honor those who have fallen."

"The simple reality of what we face is death. There is no easy way to say this. Each and every one of us must face it. That being said, there are noble deaths, and there are cowardly deaths. Those who rest here today went down the noble path. They died in service to the realms. They died trying to keep the Dark One from destroying our lives."

"I know this doesn't make it easier for any of you. These were your friends, your family, and now they are gone. There is nothing I can say that will take away your pain, and I will not try to. The simple truth is, we were attacked. For seemingly no reason, the Dark One struck the Nest. Why?

Intel? To cull our ranks? Maybe, but we believe the Dark One saw an opportunity to strike fear into our hearts, an opportunity to dull our resolve. New magics and technology are in place to prevent this from happening again. Security has been increased. We will not be caught off-guard again."

Myrddin hung his head for a second as he gathered his words. "I have asked a great deal from all of you. I understand that, and I want you to know I understand. None of you has to be here. I will not hold you prisoner to agreements made previously. Now that you have seen war, seen loss…"

Myrddin's voice cracked, and he stepped away from the podium. Roy stood up and took Myrddin's place. "I think what Myrddin is trying to say is that we ain't asking y'all to die. None of us are. What happened was terrible. We didn't see it coming. I wish we had, and honestly, these deaths are on our heads."

Toppinir nodded as Myrddin took a seat next to him. "We all lost friends," Roy continued. "Those friends died heroes. That don't make it any easier, though. Not at all. So, we're here to honor them. Here to honor their sacrifices, and those who stay will make sure those sacrifices were not made in vain."

Roy sat back down, and Toppinir stood and walked to the podium. "Now we will allow a viewing of the departed. Please feel free to pay your respects," he said softly before sitting back down.

It took a while for the cadets to rise from their seats and approach the coffins at the front of the hall. Most of the cadets were teenagers, and it was the first time they had been confronted with death. Alex was the first amongst them. She stood and marched straight to the front.

Alex wore her blindfold during the service, but she pulled it off as she headed toward the bodies up front. The light was blinding, but she forced her way through it until it felt normal. Then she looked upon the dead who had fallen for the sake of Middang3ard.

At first, Alex didn't recognize anyone, but that didn't matter. They had all been living and breathing individuals with goals and fears and loves, and now they were gone. That was what mattered.

Then Alex's eyes fell on Primerose. She was laid out with the cadets, her scales shimmering in the crystal light of the Nest. Her eyes were closed, a golden coin laid upon them like the rest of the dead. Her many arms were folded over her chest. She looked peaceful.

Alex leaned over and kissed her forehead. She didn't know what else to do. She'd had no idea Primerose had been killed in the battle, and that knowledge rocked her to the core. Alex felt like she needed to sit down. It was all becoming too much.

Alex made her way back to her seat and watched the rest of the cadets pay their respects. She saw Gill, Brath, and Jollies make their way past the cadets and instructors they knew.

Once the living cadets had paid their respects, they returned to their seats. At the podium, Myrddin stood and cleared his throat as he wiped away his tears. "Even amongst the horrors we experienced, we will always have reasons to live, to celebrate, to continue forward," he said.

"Bravery does not come easily and often is never commended. I would like to take a moment to do just that. Many of the people here are indebted to Alex Bound."

Alex's heart jumped in her chest. She stared at Myrddin, who was looking right at her. "Alex Bound," Myrddin continued, "organized a party that rescued many of our cadets. She also freed our dragons and led the final stand against the Dark One's forces."

"She was accompanied by Jollies Dust, Gill Lowborn, and Brath Gimbel. These four individuals showed bravery and valor beyond their years."

Myrddin started clapping, quickly joined by Roy and Toppinir and the rest of the instructors. The hall broke into cheers as the cadets stood up, clapping, and grabbed the four named cadets if they were close enough.

Someone hugged Alex tightly and thanked her. She didn't know what to say or do. She just stood there blank-faced, trying to determine how she felt about what was going on around her.

"Alex the Boundless saved us!"

Alex didn't know who had started the chanting. The hall was echoing her name.

Alex pushed the person who was hugging her away, then turned and ran out of the Great Hall.

Back in her room, Alex sat on her bed, trying to find words. She couldn't understand why anyone would praise her. She had just done what she should have. And so many cadets had died. Who was she to be praised?

It hurt—all of it. There was nothing she could do about it.

Alex leaned over and clutched her stomach. A searing pain had started in her bowels and was working its way through her chest up to her throat. She ran to the bathroom in her dorm and knelt over the toilet.

Boundless—that was what they were chanting, the name she used in VR. But this wasn't VR. Nothing about this was virtual. It was reality, plain and simple, and the reality was too much.

Dead orcs flashed in Alex's mind, her knife stabbing one of them—the knife that was still on her side. That knife had killed. *She* had killed. The Great Hall was full of dead cadets.

Alex's body convulsed as she threw up. Stomach acid burned her throat as she coughed and tried to pull herself up.

It didn't work. Her legs were too weak, and her entire body was trembling.

The last few days (or weeks, she didn't know) had finally caught up with her. Everything she had been pushing down, pretending it wasn't driving her crazy, came bubbling up to the surface. It needed to be gone. She needed to get it out.

Alex pulled away from the toilet and cowered in the corner as she sobbed. She tried to keep herself from crying. This was her life now.

She caught her tears in her hand and held it out. Alex had never seen herself cry. Part of her wanted to look in the mirror to see what this pain looked like.

Alex heard the door of her dorm room open and close. She jumped at the sound, worried that it might be an orc running into the room before she remembered the battle for the Nest was over. There were no orcs. It was just her roommate.

It hardly took any time to wipe her tears off and compose herself. She stared in the mirror, finally seeing herself. There were bags under her eyes from not sleeping the night before.

Alex didn't recognize her reflection, but she had only seen it a few times. *Is this me,* she wondered. *Is this who I am?*

Alex walked out of the bathroom. Jollies was waiting for her, a plate of food next to her. "I thought you might be hungry," Jollies said without meeting Alex's eyes.

Alex was hungry. She had forgotten how hungry she was. "Thank you," she managed to say.

Jollies took a deep breath before speaking. "They were chanting your name," Jollies whispered. "Alex the Boundless."

Alex forked a piece of bacon into her mouth and assumed it was obvious she couldn't talk because her mouth was full.

Jollies didn't relent. "Is that weird? I mean, do you feel weird about all that? People? Just all of it?"

Alex looked up from her food. "Yeah, I do," Alex admitted.

"It doesn't seem right. With all... With everything that happened. No one should be saying my name. All I did was try to help, and I didn't. Not enough. Not nearly enough."

Jollies fluttered over and landed on Alex's shoulder. She nestled close to Alex's ear. "I know," she said. "They were chanting my name, Gill and Brath too. It felt weird, like they shouldn't have been doing it."

"Myrddin made it sound like I saved everyone. I didn't. You saw...you saw the funeral. I didn't save anyone."

"No, you didn't."

Alex tried to focus on her food. She still couldn't get over the fact that she was seeing without Manny and not relying on the blindfold to numb her senses.

Jollies pulled Alex's ear. "You didn't save anyone. *We* did. All of us together."

Alex laughed. She didn't know where the laughter came from, but it was genuine. She couldn't express how much she appreciated Jollies at that moment. "You're right. It wasn't me. It was all of us."

"We did the best we could, and that's the important thing. We can't beat ourselves up about what we didn't or couldn't do. We did all we could."

There was a knock. Both Jollies and Alex jumped at the sound. Alex went and opened the door.

Brath and Gill were standing looking haggard and unhappy. Alex opened the door wider and motioned for them to come in. Brath sat down on Alex's bed, while Gill remained standing over by the door. "How are you guys doing?" Alex asked.

Brath pulled out his family's knife and held it in his hand. "You didn't stay for the rest of the funeral."

"I couldn't. It was all too much. I-I had to get out of there."

Brath picked at his fingernails with his knife and nodded.

"Yeah, I understand. I wish I hadn't gone. It didn't help. None of it helped."

Gill walked over to Brath and rested his hand on the gnome's shoulder. "We needed to pay our respects to the dead."

Brath leaped off the bed and pushed Gill away. "Did we?" he asked. "Did we have to see everyone we couldn't help? Did we have to lay coins on their eyes and hope they're guided to the afterlife in peace? I don't think we did. It didn't matter if we were there or not. They're *dead*."

Gill walked away from Brath and sat at Alex's desk. He hung his head, running his hands through his hair as he tried to find the right words. "We needed to be there," he said. "It was important. We can't run away from any of this."

Gill looked at Alex, his face older than Alex had ever imagined it could be. He looked as if he had aged forty years, yet he still managed to smile. "We helped. We did everything we could. That's what's important. That's all that matters."

Brath solemnly nodded as he continued to pick at his fingernails. "Yeah, I guess," he agreed. "It still feels really crappy."

Jollies flew off Alex's shoulder and flashed bright pink as she fluttered around the room. "That is the important thing, isn't it?" she asked. "Isn't that what being a dragonrider is all about? We're here to do our part. To protect the realms as much as we can. And we started doing that yesterday."

Alex knew Jollies was right deep in her heart, but that didn't make the pain go away. Maybe the pain would never leave. Maybe the pain was important, even necessary. "So, did they sing a song for us?" Alex asked. "You know, like those old odes and stuff?"

Gill laughed. "Actually, they did," he said. "Myrddin led it. It was terrible. Like, really bad. The guy cannot sing. At all.

When Roy and Toppinir took over, it got better, but none of the cadets can hold a note. You didn't miss anything."

"What now?" Alex asked. "After all this, what are we supposed to do next?"

Gill pulled down his visor and then turned it off. "We keep going. There's training tomorrow."

There was nothing Alex wanted more than a break. She didn't want to have to jump back on her dragon and continue on, yet that was what was expected of her. She was a dragonrider. That was what she was here for. "All right. What are we doing?"

# CHAPTER EIGHT

The next day, Alex rose with the sun and went to breakfast, surrounded by cadets who whispered her name as she walked by. She grabbed a seat by herself and was joined by Jollies quickly enough. Neither of them spoke much.

About half an hour into breakfast, Brath and Gill sat down at Alex's table. The four of them ate their meals in silence before getting up and leaving.

When Alex got back to her room, she checked her messages to see if she had received anything from her parents. The only message in her inbox was a reminder of the training she had to attend in an hour.

Alex laid in her bed and stared at the ceiling. She wasn't wearing her blindfold. Her sight was much better. Today might be the first day she didn't need Manny to trail behind her. Now that she thought of it, she hadn't seen Manny at breakfast.

*If anyone deserves a day off, it's that weird ball of eyes,* Alex thought.

Jollies got back to the room a little while after Alex, and

they both got dressed and ready for their training. Jollies flew over to Alex and pecked her on the cheek. "It's going to be okay," Jollies said. "We're all going to be okay."

Alex playfully nudged the pixie. "Yeah, I know. We got this."

The two left their room and made their way to the training field. The remaining cadets had already arrived, no doubt showing up early to avoid staying in their rooms and thinking about the last few days.

Brath and Gill were already on the field. They scooted over to make room for Alex.

Fier walked out onto the field. She looked tired, more tired than the cadets. "All right," she shouted. "Today, we begin a new level of your training. I'm not going to waste your time trying to play nice about what happened. I respect you all too much."

Alex felt Fier's eyes on her, and she looked at the ground. When she looked up, she saw Manny at the far end of the field. The Beholder waved one of his eye tentacles and Alex waved back.

Fier paced up and down the length of the cadets. "Truthfully, I didn't think any of us were going to survive, but here we are. Here *you* are, warriors in training. The Dark One is afraid of you. That's why we were attacked. Take it as a back-handed compliment."

Fier leapt into the air and wings spread out from her back. It was impossible to tell if she was mostly dragon or something else. "Get in the air," she shouted. "Let's get started."

Alex raised her dragon anchor to the sky and called for Chine. She looked at the sun, its dazzling brightness, the blue skies, and the sparse white clouds.

Chine came to her in a flash of black smoke, faster than

the rest of the dragons. Alex leaped onto him, and they took off.

Alex looked down at the other cadets. Many of them were still waiting for their dragons. *I'm glad we made it through everything*, Alex said to Chine. *You and me.*

Chine turned to look at Alex, his eyes dancing in a smile. *I as well*, he said. *When we were trapped, I honestly wasn't sure you and I were going to see each other again.*

*It's weird. I feel like we never really talk. I mean, not as much as everyone else I see. Not as much as Jollies or Gill or even Brath. But I feel close to you. Like, if you weren't here, maybe I wouldn't be here.*

Chine soared above the clouds as the rest of the riders started to take off. *It is the binding. It is not a thing that can be put into words simply, but we are intertwined. Nothing will change that. I am here for you. You are here for me.*

Fier and the rest of the cadets were now in the sky. Fier raised her hand and targets appeared in the air. She pointed at them and barked, "All right, everyone, get into groups of four. Take down your targets without using your dragon's elemental powers. Got it?"

Jollies, Brath, and Gill made their way toward Alex without saying anything. The four of them sized up their targets and took off.

Jollies busted through the smaller targets, Amber firing her shoulder plasma cannons. Brath was right behind her, cleaning up the larger targets. One of the targets Brath hit split into two more targets and flew away from each other,

Gill went after the two new targets. Timber swiped the targets, his mech claws tearing through both of them.

Alex was at a loss as to what to do. All the targets in her vicinity had been destroyed.

Fier came up behind Alex, sneering. "Well, it seems like

you four are far beyond target practice," she said. "How about we try something a little bit more advanced?"

Fier waved her hand and the sky disappeared. It shimmered into darkness, a darkness Alex was familiar with. *Guess it's time for VR,* Alex thought.

# CHAPTER NINE

The blackness faded and opened up into the lush world of *Middang3ard*. Alex was still atop Chine, flying through the sky amidst clouds, but the clouds were different. When Alex looked down, she could see the villages and hamlets she had grown so accustomed to in *Middang3ard*.

Brath, Gill, and Jollies were still beside Alex. Gill was looking around as if he had been dropped into a reality he didn't understand. "Where in the realms are we?" he asked.

Alex flew in front of her friends. "We're in a VR simulation," she explained. "Like the game I used to play. The game that brought me here. None of this is real. Well, not real in the sense that we can die or anything like that, but it's real enough."

Brath stared down at the world beneath him. "It almost looks like home. Almost."

Alex's heart broke for him, but before she could say anything, an icicle flew through the air, narrowly missing her head. If Chine hadn't dodged at the last minute, it would have decapitated her. "We got incoming fire!" she shouted.

Whatever had thrown the icicle was obviously not in the

air. That meant Alex needed to get to the ground as fast as possible. If their enemy could throw something that far, they must be extremely strong. "Come on," she said as she leaned forward, directing Chine toward the ground.

Her dragon rocketed toward the ground. Alex blinked back tears from the speed. This was everything she loved, yet she knew it wasn't real. Part of what she had loved about being a dragonrider was the game; this was just a reminder.

Chine and the rest of the dragons landed, throwing up dust and dirt all around them.

The four dragonrider cadets and their dragons were in front of a mountain covered in ice. Its summit was not visible, extending far into the clouds.

At the base of the mountain were twenty frost giants. They were at least ten feet tall, their lanky arms nearly scraping the ground. Ice hung from their fur, and icicles clung to their beards.

Alex leaned forward, spurring Chine onward. Chine shot a jet of ether fire at the frost giants.

The largest frost giant stepped forward and waved his hand, dispelling the fire.

Alex turned to the rest of her party and shouted, "It's rigged against us! We can't use dragon attacks!"

Brath shrugged as he pulled Furi back, trying to rein him in. "What do you mean, we can't use dragon attacks?" he asked. "Or that it's rigged against us?"

"This isn't real life. There are certain rules that whoever made this is forcing us to play by, and one of them is obviously that dragon attacks can't do anything. Gill and Jollies, get behind the giants. Brath, me and you are going to hit them head-on."

No one asked questions. In a moment of precise coordination that frankly surprised and awed Alex, Gill and Jollies swooped behind the frost giants. Brath guided Furi over to

Alex. "We have to use our weapons, just like the target practice we were doing. Come on, let's do this!"

Alex leaned forward, and Chine charged toward the frost giants.

One of the frost giants reached down and pulled up a piece of earth. The dirt instantly froze over, and the giant threw it at Chine.

Chine shot a jet of ether fire that burned through the ice. *At least the fire works for that crap*, Alex thought as Brath and Furi flew past her.

Brath fired two plasma shots. One of them hit a frost giant in the chest, vaporizing it.

Gill and Jollies were in position behind the frost giants. They both started to fire their plasma cannons.

The frost giants turned around, stunned that they were being attacked from the rear. As the confused giants tried to make sense of what was happening, Alex zeroed in on the largest and fired a volley of plasma at him.

The plasma connected with the giant and burned through his torso, instantly eviscerating him.

Jollies and Gill were firing their dragons' plasma cannons as fast as they could.

Gill leaned back, pulled up his visor, and scanned his options. He found one that worked for him and Timber and grinned as he let off a volley of missiles.

The missiles hit the center of the circle of frost giants, sending a couple of them tumbling.

As the frost giants caught up in the explosion soared through the air, Jollies swooped by using Amber's extreme speed. Lightning crackled off both of them and they shot plasma bolts, taking care of whatever giants survived Gill's initial blast.

Brath and Alex charged toward the remaining giants.

"This is over!" Alex shouted as Chine reared up on his hind legs and shot a jet of celebratory fire.

Chine chomped down on one of the frost giants, ripping it in two. "This is a battle!" He chuckled.

Gill and Jollies cut through the back end of the frost giants, their missiles and plasma cannons shearing through the icy hides of the giants. Alex and Brath took care of the remaining giants in the front of the horde. Once the smoke had settled, only the dragonriders remained.

The world broke apart for a second and the bodies of the frost giants shimmered out of existence.

Suddenly, Alex and the rest of them were back in the Wasp's Nest.

Fier walked up to the four cadets, smiling and shaking her head. "I don't know why I didn't assume you four would be the first to get through this," she said. "Wasn't expecting it to be in record time, though."

Alex smiled as she looked at Brath, Jollies, and Gill. "Yeah, well, that's how you take care of a threat." She laughed. "At least in VR. Makes it a little easier when I know I'm not going to get killed."

"And I see, no pun intended, that you didn't need to bring along your seeing-eye Beholder."

Alex hadn't even realized she hadn't brought Manny along for the ride. The thought hadn't crossed her mind. She had been looking through her own eyes the entire time. "Yeah, I guess I didn't have to," Alex muttered.

"Oh, don't go on being modest. We don't have time for that crap. We need heroes. Looks like you four might be right for the job."

## CHAPTER TEN

Alex woke up around the same time as Jollies and they both changed into their new red uniforms. Today was the day. It had come faster than Alex had assumed it would, but it was here. She was going to graduate from being a cadet to being a dragonrider.

When Jollies and Alex stepped out of their room, Gill and Brath were waiting in the hall for them. The four of them walked to the Great Hall, turned a corner to the left, and headed toward Myrddin's office.

Myrddin was waiting for them, sipping a cup of tea as he leaned back in his chair. Fier and Roy were with him. Roy stood in the corner as if he hoped to be hidden by the shadows. Fier, on the other hand, sat on top of Myrddin's desk.

There were no seats, so Alex and the rest stood at attention. She didn't know if it was appropriate since she had never been instructed to stand in such a way, but she'd read enough books to feel like it was the best decision.

Myrddin stood up, his face grave, as usual. "You all probably read the message I sent you by now," Myrddin said. "I don't see the point in repeating it. That being said, I am immensely proud of you four. Immensely. But we do not have time for congratulations."

The room started to contort, the crystal walls moving out and making room for more. Myrddin's office opened into a larger room, one as vast as the Great Hall.

Scientists zoomed by on hoverboards, checking on different computer terminals and monitors.

The monitors showed different realms. There were dozens of them, teams of scientists poring over what they were watching.

In addition to the monitors displaying the realms, there were also scrying stations. At least ten dedicated wizards stood over large bowls of water. Alex assumed they were trying to figure out what was in store for Middang3ard.

Myrddin started walking through the room, and Alex and the rest of the newly appointed dragonriders followed. "You all know we are at war," Myrddin stated. "And you four are moving to the forefront of it."

"You are the Dragonriders Boundless, second only to our first and foremost squad, which you will be backing up. Roy is in charge of that squad, the mech dragons—his idea, not mine. You will be accompanying him and his squad on their next mission."

Alex was still trying to take in everything that was happening around her. She almost didn't hear Myrddin's words. She and Gill and Brath and Jollies were part of a squad now? She had just arrived at the Wasp's Nest a few days ago.

Myrddin continued walking, and the Boundless followed him.

A staircase appeared in front of Myrddin, and he ascended it and stepped onto a platform. Manny was there, floating in front of a dozen monitors. One of his tentacled eyes flipped over and looked at the Boundless team. "We've come full circle, haven't we?" he joked.

Alex looked at the monitors. Each of them showed a different realm.

Myrddin stood next to Manny and straightened his tie. "Your mission is to accompany Roy and his Mech riders as they transport minerals and other resources to Middang3ard. These minerals will be used for weapons. It is of the utmost importance that this delivery arrives on time. I am trusting you all with this task."

The Boundless squad looked at each other. Alex was the one to speak. "You want us to do this?" she asked.

Myrddin smiled. "Yes, I do. I trust you all," he said as he turned his back to her. "And I believe I have a worthwhile addition for you."

Myrddin waved his hand, and the monitors disappeared. In their place was a floating platform.

It was Jim, her former partner in *Middang3ard* VR, waving and smiling like a dork. He was outfitted in the armor of the dragonriders. "Hey, guys," he exclaimed before turning to Alex and saying, "Long time no see!"

Alex and her team of Boundless get their first mission. A routine escort job. Thing about Middang3ard - nothing is routine. Join them on their adventure in *First Mission*.

# AUTHOR NOTES RAMY VANCE

## JANUARY 30, 2020

I started writing rather late in life, and in that time and I had failed a lot. Failed businesses, relationships ... but failing at failing?

Seriously, what kind of loser am I?

You see, before I started taking my writing seriously, I thought it would be cool to do a blog about failing. I figured that that only way to really learn is to fail. And not just fail – fail fast and often.

I learned a lot about myself in all the things I tried and did not succeed at. More than I care to share. So I started this website/blog called: Who Fails Wins. Check it out here. The video is pretty cool.

The goal was to get 100 stories about failure. If I got it, I'd start the blog.

I got 34. And most of the stories weren't really fail stories, but rather stories about sort of failing. Things like: I failed my French test, studied real hard, tried again and passed.

Not really a fail story.

But a few people took it seriously, and since this failed

endeavour deserves to be shared, I thought I'd share the top three stories. The first one is from me.

I held back the name of the other two, but know that all three stories are real – and from people who felt real pain for something that they carried/will carry with them for their whole lives.

Sorry to be such a downer on this one, but as someone who knows that stories heal, maybe stories about failure will have their strange, healing benefits, too.

**My Story – Never Said It Out Loud:**

I quit my job to take care of my dying father. It took nine months for the cancer to take him and in all that time, in all those hospital visits, all the hanging out we did watching old movies or chatting, I never once told him that I loved him. I thought about it, but for reasons I don't quite understand, I just never did. He probably knew, but I still wish had said it out loud. Even if only once.

**Fail Story 2 – Never Letting Go:**

I am 89 years old and have two children who are almost senior citizens themselves. My failure is never letting go of the pain of the loss of what would have been my second child. He was a still born that I named Michael and he is buried in my Church cemetery. When I go, I have asked my daughter to spread my ashes on the grave of a child that I never heard cry.

**Fail Story 3 – Nagging Dreams:**

Since I was 12 I've wanted to be an artist. I studied art and got my degree. I had to decide if I had the courage to be a full-time artist depending on sales. I opted for the path of least resistance, teaching. I never gave up my art or my dream of being a renowned artist which I never achieved. Failure? I now have an adequate pension for retirement. I had a family life and raised a son. I still do my art and I participate in group and solo shows. BUT my elusive dream still nags me.

# AUTHOR NOTES MICHAEL ANDERLE

FEBRUARY 1, 2020

Seriously Ramy? Failure? *Damn you, man!*

Thank you for reading our words, but I *JUST* read Ramy's *Author Notes*. I usually go along with the theme of my collaborator's *Author Notes* to keep us whole, but then he went and chose to write about failing.

Which was my business life to a degree before I failed to fail.

They say a person who succeeds is often enough not the best, but the one stubborn asshat who just never understood the concept of quitting. When the dust settled, he or she was the one there picking up their pick and slamming it into the mountain again, going after the dream.

That is me.

I was not a storyteller from a young age, crafting stories on notebooks through my teen years and receiving dozens of rejections (hundreds or thousands.) Nope. I quit. I failed.

I ran with my torn heart, ripped to pieces by well-considered opinions not willing to see the gems of encouragement on my...well, actually on me.

I tried *ONE* time to send in a story to my high school

literary magazine and was rejected. I enjoyed that so much I stole my manuscript out of the slush pile, hid it in my backpack, and never submitting anything again until thirty-two years later.

And that submission was to Amazon.

*Ad Aeternitatem, baby!*

**Diary: Sunday Jan 26ᵗʰ – Saturday Feb 1ˢᵗ**

First, the fun part. WOOT, *Goth Drow*! It's a new series I'm happy about, and it will be coming to you in early March as one of our LMBPN Large Releases of about 180k words.

Like *Witch of the Federation* or *The Steel Dragon* size.

This week, I spoke with ALLI (Alliance of Independent Authors) on a recorded video call for their symposium on selling foreign rights (with others, including Judith Anderle, our CMO for the company, who honestly spoke the most for LMBPN since it's her area of expertise.)

I finished a book titled **In Cold Type** by Leonard Shatzkin, written in 1983. The book helped open my eyes to the issues in the bookselling business. I hope to figure out a way and implement a solution for selling paperbacks (which is about .02% of our income, if that much.)

I greenlit (well, maybe only in my mind) *Cryptid Assassin 05*... but don't have a clue on where I want the story to go yet.

*(I might want to get on that.)*

Before I do that, I have two story beats to review and approve and *Opus 5* editing to finish.

I've been ill for the last forty-eight hours and had to learn to respect my body once again. It has probably been twelve months or longer that I have gone without any serious sick downtime. There is nothing like experience to foster sympathy through empathy, at least for me.

There is going to be a big author signing/fan get together

or something going on the Friday after the 20Booksto50k Event here in Las Vegas in November (the show runs Tuesday to Thursday 10th-12th). Yes, yes, I know that is Friday the 13th ;-). I didn't set the date—ask Martelle about that one! The event will be held at Sam's Town Casino and Hotel (about twenty minutes east of the Strip driving straight over.)

For those who know, I'm doing a weight loss "thing" with my older brother. My goal was to be under 220 by Feb 1st. I weighed in at 218.8.

Go, Team! (I imagine being sick and unable to eat much helped, but what the hell. I'm keeping that W on my side.) I need to finish on June 30th at UNDER 202.0 lbs. If it looks like I might miss it, you may see Anderle doing all sorts of crazy stuff to drop weight.

I'm going to wrap up this diary post since I'm about two days past due on a lot of work. Take care of yourselves, and I'll chat with you in the next... OH OH!

New Universe coming 2020! (Well, uh, that's not even a big deal anymore—it's LMBPN. *OF COURSE, THERE IS A NEW UNIVERSE COMING!*)

Enjoy.

Michael Anderle

# OTHER BOOKS BY THE AUTHORS

**Other Middang3ard Books**

Never Split The Party (01)
Late To the Party (02)
It's My Party (03)
Blue Hell And Alien Fire (04)

Death Of An Author: A Middang3ard Novella

**Other Books by Ramy Vance**

Mortality Bites Series
Keep Evolving Series
Fatebound Series

**Other Books by Michael Anderle**

For a complete list of books by Michael Anderle, please visit:

**www.lmbpn.com/ma-books/**

All LMBPN Audiobooks are Available at Audible.com and iTunes. To see all LMBPN audiobooks, including those written by Michael Anderle please visit:

**www.lmbpn.com/audible**

## CONNECT WITH THE AUTHORS

**Connect with Ramy**

Join Ramy's Newsletter

Join Ramy's FB Group: House of the GoneGod Damned!

**Connect with Michael Anderle and sign up for his email list here:**

Website: http://lmbpn.com

Email List: http://lmbpn.com/email/

Facebook:
www.facebook.com/TheKurtherianGambitBooks

www.ingramcontent.com/pod-product-compliance
Lightning Source LLC
Chambersburg PA
CBHW022023120726
47898CB00008BA/2835